A Mother's Song

by Janet Lawler

illustrated by Kathleen Kemly

STERLING

New York / London

I'll slow down my footsteps
and sing a sweet song.
We'll share nature's wonders
as we walk along.

Come kneel by the pathway
and sift through the sand.
You'll find silver pebbles,
and gold, in your hand.

Let's wade in a puddle
that's not very deep,
pretending we're frogs,
croaking loud as we leap.

Listen with me
to the happiest birds
calling, "Good morning!"
with chirp-chirping words.

Bend by the garden
and sniff, one by one,
the blossoms that burst
in the warmth of the sun.

Feel summer showers
fall cool on our toes,
before running off
to wherever rain goes.

Chase after leaves
floating down from the trees.
They're dancing in circles
like lost bumblebees.

The apples we harvest
together taste best,
and yours crunches louder
than all of the rest.

Snowflakes land softly
to tickle your face,
as we flop on our backs,
making angels in place.

The pond's frozen over,
it's slippery-slick.
Hug me and twirl
in a slow spinning trick.

With your hand holding mine,
I'm so happy to share
the magic that's here,
all around, everywhere.

STERLING and the distinctive Sterling logo are registered trademarks of
Sterling Publishing Co., Inc.

Library of Congress Cataloging-in-Publication Data

Lawler, Janet.
A mother's song / by Janet Lawler ; illustrated by Kathleen Kemly.
p. cm.
Summary: A mother finds special ways to enjoy nature with her child all through the year.
ISBN 978-1-4027-6968-9
[1. Stories in rhyme. 2. Mother and child--Fiction. 3. Nature--Fiction.]
I. Kemly, Kathleen Hadam, ill. II. Title.
PZ8.3.L355Mot 2010
[E]--dc22

2009027239

Lot # :
2 4 6 8 10 9 7 5 3 1
11/09
Published by Sterling Publishing Co., Inc.
387 Park Avenue South, New York, NY 10016
© 2010 by Janet Lawler
Illustrations © 2010 by Kathleen Kemly
The illustrations in this book were created with pastels.
Distributed in Canada by Sterling Publishing
c/o Canadian Manda Group, 165 Dufferin Street,
Toronto, Ontario, Canada M6K 3H6

Sterling ISBN 978-1-4027-6968-9

For information about custom editions, special sales, premium and
corporate purchases, please contact Sterling Special Sales
Department at 800-805-5489 or specialsales@sterlingpublishing.com.

Designed by Mina Chung.

To Andy, my nature lover, and Cami,
my lover of life.
—J.L.

Remembering Nancy, sitting on the porch at the
Vineyard watching the roses bloom.
—K.K.